Mr. Yowder
and the
Train Robbers

Weekly Reader Books presents

Mr. Yowder
and the
Train Robbers

WRITTEN AND ILLUSTRATED BY
GLEN ROUNDS

Holiday House, New York

This book is a presentation of
Weekly Reader Books.

Weekly Reader Books offers
book clubs for children from
preschool through junior high school.
All quality hardcover books are selected by
a distinguished Weekly Reader Selection Board.

For further information write to:
Weekly Reader Books
1250 Fairwood Ave.
Columbus, Ohio 43216

Copyright © 1981 by Glen Rounds
All rights reserved
Printed in the United States of America

Library of Congress Cataloging in Publication Data

Rounds, Glen, 1906—
    Mr. Yowder and the train robbers.

    Summary: Relates how Mr. Yowder outwits a gang of
bank robbers with the help of some friendly rattlesnakes.
    [1. West(U.S.)—Fiction.   2. Snakes—Fiction.
3. Robbers and outlaws—Fiction.   4. Humorous stories]
I. Title.
PZ7.R761M   [Fic]   81-2198
ISBN 0-8234-0394-7   AACR2

Mr. Xenon Zebulon Yowder's famous adventure with the gang of train robbers happened many, many years ago when the country was, in some respects, wilder than it is now—and train robbery much more common.

But over the years, through many tellings and retellings, the story has become garbled beyond recognition. There are folk who are firmly convinced that Mr. Yowder was himself a member of the gang. And there are others just as firmly convinced that, instead, Mr. Yowder faced the desperados in a shoot-out, and singlehandedly laid them all low.

The truth, however, as so often happens, lies somewhere in between. And here, for the first time, is the true and unadorned account of what actually did occur—how the adventure came about, and how it ended, as well as a detailed description of the part the twenty-seven rattlesnakes played in the affair.

Mr. Yowder, who claimed to be "The World's Bestest and Fastest Sign Painter," would probably never have gotten involved with the train robber gang if it hadn't been for his meeting with Mr. Pernell P. Hagadorn.

Mr. Hagadorn was not a train robber nor, as far as anyone knows, did he even know any such. At the time we speak of he owned an overall factory, making overalls that were said to wear like elephant hide. And he wanted Mr. Yowder to paint life-sized elephants on the sides of barns and stores across the state of Kansas to advertise his product.

But Mr. Yowder liked variety in his work—something different every day—so he told Mr. Hagadorn that the idea of spending the summer painting the same sign over and over didn't appeal to him.

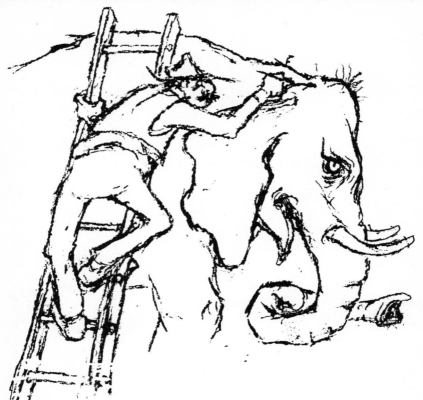

Mr. Hagadorn, however, said that to make the job more interesting, Mr. Yowder could change the elephant's expression from time to time, or have him facing in different directions. And, besides, he would pay him very well.

So in the end Mr. Yowder agreed to take the job.

All through that summer he painted elephants day after day, no two alike. Some looked fierce and some looked kindly, some faced east and some faced west, but all were magnificent beasts, and were much admired by passing farmers and tourists for years afterwards.

By the middle of August there wasn't a store or barn anywhere in Kansas that didn't have an elephant painted on it. And when Mr. Hagadorn paid Mr. Yowder off, he was so pleased with the job that he gave him a few dollars extra as a bonus.

With all that money in his pocket, Mr. Yowder thought he would take a little vacation to sort of rest up from painting elephants all summer. The lady who ran the boardinghouse told him there was good fishing back in the hills south of town. So right after supper, Mr. Yowder, who purely loved to fish, hurried across the street to the hardware store and bought himself a fish pole and some hooks. And next morning he rode out a few miles on a rancher's wagon and dropped off where a clear stream crossed the road.

The stream ran through some of the roughest country Mr. Yowder had ever seen, but by noon he had caught a nice mess of fish. So he built a fire in a little clearing and cooked some of the smaller ones for his dinner.

After he'd eaten, Mr. Yowder lay back on the soft grass and took himself a nap. When he woke it was well along in the afternoon, so he gathered up his things and started looking about for a shortcut back to the main road.

But he had gone only a little distance when, coming out from between two low hills, he found himself at the head of a weed-grown street running between the tumbledown buildings of a long-abandoned settlement.

The old-fashioned false fronts leaned at crazy angles and there were great holes in most of the sagging roofs and porches. But when he was over his first surprise, Mr. Yowder cautiously explored the nearest buildings. He found a few rusting cans, and the usual litter of old magazines and papers, but otherwise there was no sign that anyone had visited the place for years.

The sign across the front of the old hotel had not entirely weathered away, and the roof over what had been the lobby didn't seem to leak too badly. So Mr. Yowder decided it would be a good place to camp for a few days while he caught up on his fishing. The only well he'd found had no water in it, just some trash and the rickety ladder the long-forgotten well digger hadn't bothered to pull out of the hole when he abandoned the job. But Mr. Yowder figured he could carry what water he needed from the creek.

So, dragging a broken chair out onto the porch, he sat a while, admiring the view before starting back to the boardinghouse and supper.

Next morning when he rode out of town with the mail carrier, Mr. Yowder was carrying a couple of blankets, a frying pan, and several days' supply of coffee, bacon, and some canned goods stuffed into a grain sack.

Back at the abandoned town, he swept out the lobby of the old hotel, arranged his plunder, and checked to see that the rusty stove was in working order. Then he dug a can of worms and hurried to the creek.

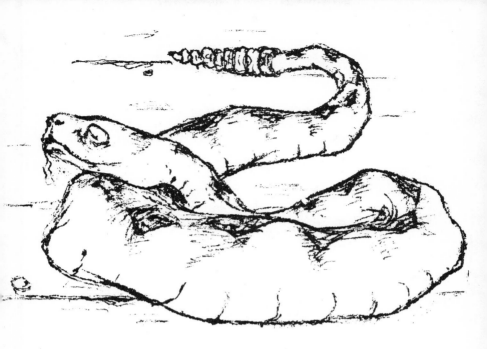

When he came back around noon with another nice mess of fish, the biggest rattlesnake he'd ever seen was sunning himself on the hotel porch.

The snake started down through a hole in the porch floor, but Mr. Yowder spoke to him in Snake— you probably remember that Mr. Yowder had learned to speak Snake down in Oklahoma some years before— and asked him to wait up a minute.

As might be expected, the rattlesnake was somewhat surprised at hearing his language spoken. But he waited politely while Mr. Yowder explained that he just wanted to camp in the building for a few days, and would try to be as little trouble as possible.

The snake said it had been a long time since he'd had anyone to talk to, or had heard any news, and that Mr. Yowder was welcome to stay around as long as he liked.

So Mr. Yowder dragged a chair out onto the porch and read the snake the more interesting bits from a newspaper he happened to have in his pocket. Between items the snake told Mr. Yowder about his sleeping place under the building, and of the small happenings in the town.

It was sundown almost before they knew it, and Mr. Yowder asked the snake to stay and have a bite of supper with him.

The snake thanked him, but said he had a broken fang that made his mouth so sore he couldn't eat. However, he would take a small saucer of cold coffee and condensed milk, if it wasn't too much trouble.

But Mr. Yowder had done considerable simple dentistry and, after asking the snake to open wide, he quickly smoothed and rounded the jagged end of the broken fang with the little file he carried in his pocket for sharpening fishhooks.

When he'd finished, the snake ran his tongue over the place and said it felt as good as new, and maybe he would have a little supper after all.

The weather stayed fine, and Mr. Yowder went fishing every morning, but in the afternoons he and the snake talked or took naps on the sunny porch. One day when the wind was blowing scraps of paper across the porch floor, the snake found what he thought must be a picture of one of his skinny relatives.

Mr. Yowder explained that the paper was a page from an old Boy Scout handbook, and the picture was simply a diagram showing how to tie a square knot. Not having any string or rope handy, he took the snake's tail in one hand, and his neck in the other and loosely tied them together to show how it was done.

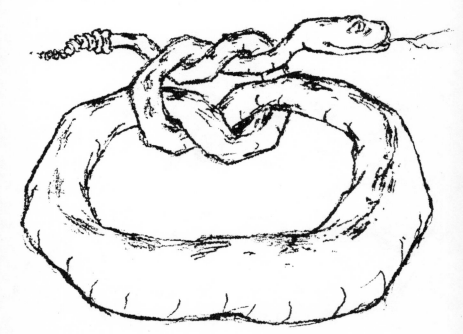

The old rattlesnake was very pleased with the trick, and practiced tying and untying the knot himself. At first, as most people do, he sometimes ended up with a slipknot instead, but before long he was able to tie it right every time.

Later he invented a sort of game. After tying himself into a loop he'd roll down the street hoopsnake fashion. Said it was the most fun he'd had in years!

Then one evening when Mr. Yowder and the old snake were inside fixing an early supper, four strangers rode up to the end of the street and stopped their horses.

They were dangerous-looking men, unshaven and with pistols in their belts and rifles in saddle scabbards.

"This is the hideout I told you about," the leader said. "Nobody's been here for years. We'll rob the train at Alkali Springs tomorrow, and come back here for a day or two while we rest and divide the loot. The sheriff will never think of looking for us here."

Then one of the riders behind him pointed to the smoke coming out of the old hotel chimney. "Somebody's already found the hideout," he said. "Let's get out of here!"

The leader looked again. "I don't see any sign of horses," he said after a little. "It may just be some old prospector or some such. Let's take a look."

So, with their hands on their guns, they rode cautiously up to the edge of the old porch.

When he heard the horses, Mr. Yowder looked out through the broken window, then turned to the snake and said, "You'd better get out of sight. I don't like the looks of those jaspers."

When the old rattlesnake had slithered down through a hole in the floor, Mr. Yowder stepped outside and told the strangers "Howdy."

The leader explained to Mr. Yowder that they were stock buyers just passing through the country, and wondered if they could stay the night.

Even though they didn't look like stock buyers to him, Mr. Yowder told the man they were welcome, and suggested that they camp down by the creek where there was water for their horses.

But the leader dismounted and pushed rudely past Mr. Yowder, looked around, then remarked that since Mr. Yowder was all alone, they'd just throw their beds down inside and keep him company.

"It's all right," the leader told the others when he went outside. "The old man is alone, so we'll keep close watch on him tonight and figure what to do with him in the morning."

Mr. Yowder was sure he'd seen pictures of the strangers on reward posters somewhere, and figured that as soon as they went to sleep, he'd sneak out and go for the sheriff. But the men kept the lantern burning all night, and every time Mr. Yowder stirred, he found one or another of them awake and watching him.

In the morning the strangers were up early, and the one that went out to bring up the horses told the leader about the old well outside. "That's just the place for you, old man," the leader said to Mr. Yowder. "We've got to rob a train today, and we'd like to be sure you'll be right here when we come back tonight."

So they made Mr. Yowder climb down into the well, and when he was on the bottom, they pulled the ladder up and threw it on the ground.

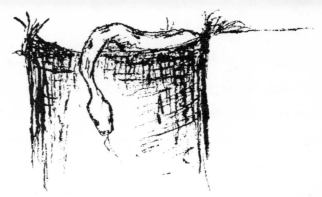

Mr. Yowder listened to the robbers ride away, then sat down (there wasn't room for him to pace around) and wondered what would become of him.

It was well after sunup when some pebbles rattled down from above and he found the old snake looking over the edge of the well. The snake hissed something but, as all snakes do, he had a very soft voice and Mr. Yowder couldn't make out what he was saying even when he'd repeated it. So, after nodding a couple of times, the snake pulled his head back and disappeared.

Then Mr. Yowder felt lonelier than ever.

He knew there was no way the snake could help him out of his predicament, but it would have been nice if he'd have stayed around just to look over the edge now and again.

All forenoon he sat there while the sunlight crept slowly down the wall. Noon came, with the sun shining straight down to the bottom of the well, but still there was no sign of his only friend, the old rattlesnake.

Mr. Yowder grew more and more discouraged.

But sometime late in the afternoon, Mr. Yowder began hearing small scufflings and hissings from above.

This went on for some time, then some bits of dirt fell on his hat. Looking up he saw the head of a strange rattlesnake slowly coming into sight at the top of the well. When half his body was in sight, the snake stopped moving and for a while simply hung head downwards against the wall.

After some more small noises from somewhere out of sight, the strange snake again started moving downwards, inch by inch. Then the head of another strange snake appeared behind the first. Mr. Yowder could scarcely believe his eyes when he saw that the two were tied together, neck to tail, in a perfect square knot!

There were many delays, but one after another, snake after snake wriggled into sight—each one's neck tied to the tail of the one ahead.

Before long the knotted rope of well-muscled rattlesnakes hung nearly to the bottom of the well. The nearest snake, seeing that he was easily within Mr. Yowder's reach, hissed to the one above, "Far enough! Pass it on."

From snake to snake the word was passed upwards to the ones out of sight at the top.

And after short delay word from somewhere above was passed back down again, "Tell him to climb up."

Taking a firm hold of the nearest snake's body, Mr. Yowder tugged a couple of times to make sure the line was securely anchored. Then, spitting on his hands, he climbed up hand over hand, and soon scrambled safely out on top.

Mr. Yowder found the old rattlesnake tied to the end of the line, with his tail wrapped several times around a nearby post. Telling him to hang on just a minute more, Mr. Yowder quickly pulled the others back out of the well, coiling them neatly on the grass as he did so.

His weight had pulled the knots so tight the snakes were unable to undo them, and it took Mr. Yowder a half hour or more to get them untied from one another.

When the snakes had finished stretching the kinks out of their necks and tails, Mr. Yowder invited them all up to the hotel for cold coffee and condensed milk. There was plenty of coffee left in the pot the robbers had made for their breakfast, and he found several unopened cans of condensed milk among their supplies.

The snakes waited politely while Mr. Yowder filled some old saucers and set them on the floor, but when he waved a hand and said "Drink up!," they didn't hesitate. Three or four to the saucer, they began thirstily lapping up milk and coffee.

While the snakes were busy with their snacks, Mr. Yowder—being careful not to step on their tails—paced up and down the room, thinking.

When everyone was finished he told them all how much he appreciated their help in getting him out of the well.

The old rattlesnake said it wasn't anything, really. He'd simply happened to think of the square-knot trick and passed the word among his neighbors.

Then Mr. Yowder went on to say there most surely would be a large reward offered for the train robbers, and he'd figured out a way to capture them, if the snakes were willing to help him one more time.

After he had carefully explained his plan, the snakes talked it over among themselves, then said they'd be right pleased to help him out. It was years since anything exciting had happened in the neighborhood, and catching a band of robbers would make an even better story than their pulling Mr. Yowder out of the well. They'd probably even get their pictures in the paper.

Then a snake they called Joe spoke up and said that he'd purely like to help capture the robbers, but he thought he'd strained his back that afternoon. Mr. Yowder said not to worry, the other snakes could handle the job without trouble, and for Joe to go along home and take it easy for a a day or two.

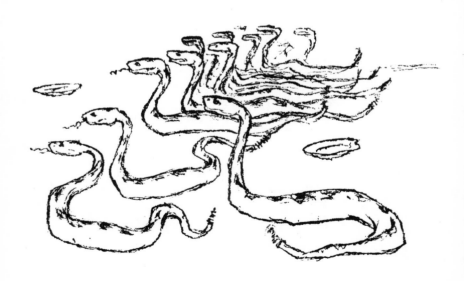

By that time it was beginning to get dark, and they heard the robbers' horses outside. The snakes disappeared through holes in the floor, and Mr. Yowder hid himself in a little closet under the old stairs just as the robbers stomped in, dragging several heavy mailbags, and an iron Wells Fargo chest.

They seemed to be in fine spirits, and from their loud talk, Mr. Yowder discovered that after they'd held up the train, they had robbed the passengers as well as the mail car.

The leader lit the lantern and emptied one of the sacks on the table. "We'll count the express car money later," he said. "But first let's see what we got off the passengers."

As soon as the robbers were busy sorting through the pile of loot, trying on diamond rings, selecting gold watches and watch chains and fancy stickpins, Mr. Yowder signaled the snakes by tapping twice, softly, on the floor with his boot heel.

The robbers were so busy with their loot they didn't notice the soft scaly rustlings as the rattlesnakes came up through the holes in the old floor and gathered in a circle around the table.

When they were all in their places, Mr. Yowder stepped quietly out of the closet and said, "Don't move, gents, until you've taken a good look at what's down by your feet."

They did as he said, and saw big rattlesnakes in the patches of lamplight while beady eyes and white fangs glittered in the shadows around their feet. And then, to add to their fright, the terrible buzzing of twenty-six sets of rattles suddenly filled the room.

One robber fainted but another caught him before he could fall down among the snakes.

Mr. Yowder told them that as long as they stood real still the snakes wouldn't bite them. So they stood REAL still while he gathered up all their guns and carried them out to the well and threw them in.

When he came back he pushed some broken chairs up to the table and told the robbers to make themselves comfortable. He said they could play cards if they wanted, providing they didn't make any quick moves to annoy the snakes, who buzzed and showed their fangs whenever a robber stirred.

None of them seemed to want to play cards. They just sat there glaring at one another all through the night, while Mr. Yowder dozed in his chair or thought about the fine reward he'd surely get for capturing the robber gang and returning all their loot.

When the sun came up, Mr. Yowder yawned and said, "Well, let's go to town and see the sheriff."

He told two of the unhappy robbers to each take a handle of the Wells Fargo chest while the others carried the heavy canvas bags. Then with rattlesnakes crawling in front, on either side, and behind them, they stumbled along the old road.

The robber leader complained that his feet hurt, and asked if they couldn't ride their horses. But Mr. Yowder told him that walking was fine exercise and, besides, they'd have no use for horses where they were going.

By the time they climbed the last rocky hill and came out onto the main road, the complaining robbers were footsore and out of breath, so Mr. Yowder let them stop for a little rest.

After making sure the circle of snakes was carefully guarding them, he looked towards the town and noticed a high, fast-moving cloud of dust rapidly moving his way. As it came closer he saw under it a big posse of mounted men riding at a gallop behind the sheriff, whose white hat and gold badge glittered in the sun.

Telling the rattlesnakes and the robbers to stay where they were, Mr. Yowder—with a big smile on his face—stepped out into the middle of the road and held up his hand.

But the posse neither slowed not stopped. As they came nearer, the sound of the horses' hooves drowned out the fierce buzzing of the rattlesnakes, and at the last minute Mr. Yowder had to dive for the ditch to avoid being ridden down.

As he thundered past on his foam-flecked horse, the sheriff hollered, "Can't stop now. We're looking for the train robbers! THERE'S A BIG REWARD!"

After the posse had passed and the thick cloud of dust had finally settled, Mr. Yowder looked around and found himself alone.

To save themselves from being trampled by the horses, the rattlesnakes had scattered into the high grass, for which Mr. Yowder could not really blame them. And finding themselves unguarded, the train robbers had snatched up their loot and scuttled back into the thick brush at the bottom of the rocky slope.

There was no way Mr. Yowder could catch them again, so after a while he dusted himself off and walked on into town. When he got there the Denver train was just pulling in, so he bought himself a ticket and climbed aboard.

He often wondered, in years afterwards, if the robbers were ever caught, and if they were, who got the reward he so nearly collected.

And that is the TRUE STORY of Mr. Yowder's adventure with the train robber gang.